Play It Safe

A Book About Safety All Year Round

By Joan Webb

Illustrated by Terri Super

Prepared with the cooperation of Bernice Berk, Ph.D.,
of the Bank Street College of Education

A GOLDEN BOOK · NEW YORK

Western Publishing Company, Inc., Racine, Wisconsin 53404

Note to Parents

Children are introduced to the concept of safety when they're very young, and all those rules can seem a little confusing. Parents can support the learning process by judging how much their children can handle, and by trying to build safety consciousness slowly and carefully.

This book offers a good way to start. The text gives safety information for situations that children are familiar with, such as riding in a car or bus, crossing the street, and observing traffic signals, as well as for playtime activities throughout the year. There is a short verse for each safety rule. You may find that you can make the book more enjoyable by saying the rules with your child. Point out the safety features shown in the illustrations as you go along. Of course, this book is only an introduction, and your child may encounter situations that are not covered here. Always be responsive to your child's questions about safety, and take the time to answer them. Remember that part of your responsibility to your child is to teach him or her the importance of personal safety.

Children learn by example. When you take a safety precaution at home, such as clearing the stairs and hallways of toys so that no one will trip, explain to your child why you're doing it. When your child sees you practicing a safety rule, it will become more real to him or her—and more likely to be remembered.

It's smart to be safe. Help your child to realize this, and to make safety awareness a natural part of his or her life.

—The Editors

Play it safe
While having fun
In winter snow
Or summer sun.
In springtime
Or when fall is here,
Play it safe
Throughout the year!

In the rain,
The sun, or snow,
There are some things
That you should know.

On a drive
In any weather,
Keep your seat belt
Snapped together.

In a store
Or on the street,
Don't talk to strangers
You may meet.

Traffic lights
And stop signs, too,
Are there to tell us
What to do.

Red means STOP,
And green means GO;
A yellow light means
Take it SLOW.

Play it safe—
Don't cross without
A grown-up there
To help you out.

No matter what
The weather's like,
Be careful when
You're on your bike.

Stay only where
Your parents say
It's safe for you
To ride and play.

Spring is here,
The weather's great,
So go outside
And roller skate.

But play it safe,
And don't take spills,
Stay clear of
Bumpy roads and hills.

At the park
Please stay away
From swings and slides
While others play.

If it's not safe,
Then stand aside
Until it's your turn
For a ride.

On jungle gyms,
Don't climb too high;
Remember this:
You can't fly!

Summer is fun,
But stick to the rules
Whenever you're at
Beaches or pools.

Play it safe—
Make sure you know
A grown-up's there,
Then in you go!

Don't swim far
Whatever you do,
The water might be
Too deep for you.

No matter what
You think or wish,
You're still a kid—
Not a fish!

Life jackets are
Great summer coats,
They'll keep you safe
On ships and boats.

While on a hike,
Don't stop to munch
Forest berries
For your lunch.

Beware of plants
With leaves of three,
For poison ivy
It may be!

Fall is here,
And all around
Leaves are drifting
To the ground.

Raking leaves
Is lots of fun,
But put the rakes back
When you're done.

Play it safe
Is still the rule
Now that it is
Time for school.

On the bus
Stay in your seat,
You're much safer
Off your feet!

Wintertime,
The time is right
To build a snowman,
Frosty white.

So bundle up
From head to toe,
Stay warm while playing
In the snow.

Play it safe
And use your head,
Think before
You ride your sled.

If trees or rocks
Are in the way,
Find a safer
Place to play.

Play it safe—
Don't fool around
When snow and ice
Are on the ground.

Icy patches
On the street
Can quickly sweep you
Off your feet.

Now you know
Just what to do
To play it safe
The whole year through!